This book belongs to :

.............Ashley Elizabeth ahl.......................

PUBLISHED BY PETER HADDOCK LIMITED,
BRIDLINGTON, ENGLAND
PRINTED IN ITALY

ISBN O 7105 0377 6

THREE LITTLE PIGS

The three little pigs lived with their mother on the edge of the wood. One day, the mother pig decided that they were too big for her little house and that it was time for them to go and build houses of their own. Just before they went, their mother gave them a stern warning about the wolf. She said that the wolf was very sly and would try to find a way of catching the little pigs to eat them. The little pigs promised to watch out for the wolf and set off to start building.

"We must all build strong houses to keep out the wolf," said one little pig.

"I shall build my house from straw," said the second little pig.

The third little pig didn't answer, he was busy watching a butterfly go past. He thought that the first little pig was making a fuss about nothing.

"We shall be safe enough," he thought.

Soon the house of straw was built. It looked very nice but the second little pig thought he would build his house with wood which was a lot stronger. The eldest little pig helped his brother to build his house of wood, as he had helped with the house of straw. He was very good at building and a few hours later, the house of wood was finished.

The next day, work was started on the third house. The eldest little pig knew that it would take more than wood and straw to keep out the wolf so he chose bricks to build his house with. Unfortunately, the little pig's brothers were too busy playing to help him build his house so it took much, much longer to finish.

The poor little pig had no house now so he ran as fast as he could to his brother's house.

"Quick, quick, let me in, the wolf is after me!" cried the first little pig.

"Come inside and hide with me," replied his brother.

This time, the wolf didn't blow the house down straight away. He waited nearby until the little pigs came outside. Suddenly, they spotted the wolf hiding nearby and the little pigs ran into the house.
They were too fast for the wolf.
"Let me in, little pigs," said the wolf through the letter box.
"By the hair on our chinny chin chins, we'll not let you in," replied the pigs.
"Then I'll blow your house down!"
And he did.

The two little pigs ran to their brother's house nearby.
"Please let us in," they said as the wolf got closer and closer.
So the eldest little pig let his brothers into his safe,
strong house made of bricks.

"I'll huff and I'll puff and I'll blow your house down," shouted the wolf.
"We won't let you in, wolf," laughed the little pigs, knowing that they were safe in the brick house.
So the wolf huffed and puffed, and huffed and puffed, until he was worn out and had no puff left.

The wolf had found a ladder and was now up on the roof.
"I'll climb on your roof and come down the chimney to eat you!" called the wolf in a rage.

"Quick, let's build up the fire," said the eldest pig. "Pass me some more logs, please."
There was soon a huge fire in the grate and the little pigs sat down to wait for the
wolf.

Little did the wolf know what was in store for him!
First his tail appeared, then one foot and then the three little pigs heard a great roar.
"Aaaahh!"

With that, the wolf climbed up the chimney twice as fast as he had come down it, there were flames leaping from his tail.

What a rage he was in now! His shouts could be heard in the village miles away and people wondered what was happening.

The little pigs thought that it was the funniest thing they had ever seen. They laughed and laughed-until tears ran down their faces.

The poor wolf ran as fast as he could to the stream nearby and doused the flames in the water.

Then, the eldest little pig decided that it was time the other two houses were rebuilt.

"And this time, we'll make them from bricks," he said.

So all three pigs set to work to build the houses of bricks to make sure that the wolf could never again blow their houses down.

THE END